FR- 20525
LE

Granny Sarah and the last Red Kite

Malachy Doyle

Illustrated by Petra Brown

PONT

To my eldest brother, David, historian and bird-watcher – M.D.

For Mum and Dad – P.B.

Published in 2006 by Pont Books, an imprint of
Gomer Press, Llandysul, Ceredigion SA44 4JL

ISBN 1 84323 677 X
ISBN-13 9781843236771
A CIP record for this title is available from the British Library

Thanks to Leigh Denyer and his colleagues at Bwlch Nant yr Arian
for their advice in the preparation of this book.

This book is published with the financial support of the
Welsh Books Council.

Printed and bound in Wales at
Gomer Press, Llandysul, Ceredigion SA44 4JL

Granny Sarah's cottage, high in the Welsh hills, is Lowri's favourite place in all the world.

Her favourite sight in all the world is the red kite, soaring over the fields and valleys. She loves its long forked tail, the way it glides with wings spread wide to the wind, and its high lonely call.

And Lowri's favourite story, in all the world by far, is the one about how Granny Sarah saved the last red kite in Wales.

'Tell me again, Granny,' Lowri asks, every time she comes to stay. 'Tell me about the kites.'

Granny Sarah makes a pot of tea, puts another log on the fire and pulls her chair up close.

'Long ago,' she begins, 'there were red kites all over Britain . . .

'In those days
they didn't just
live in the forests and
mountains − they were everywhere!

'It's said they were so tame that they would take bread and
butter from the hands of children. And the king passed a law
saying that no one was to hurt them because they helped to keep
the streets of London clean.'

7

'So what happened, Granny?'
Lowri asks, sucking on a ginger
biscuit. She knows the story
back to front but she always
wants to hear it again. 'Why did
they nearly disappear?'

'Oh,' says Granny, scowling, 'some people didn't like them at all. Farmers thought they killed too many chickens, and gamekeepers said they took their young birds. They shot them and poisoned them and once the kites became rare, people began to steal their eggs. They were driven out of the towns and villages, hunted deep into the hills, and a hundred years ago the last red kites in England and Scotland were gone.'

'But there were still some here in Wales,
weren't there, Granny?' Lowri
helps herself to another biscuit.

'Yes, cariad. But by the time I was your age, there
were hardly any left. Not that we noticed, up here on the
farm, for there'd always been kites round about. But one
day a man came and told us that the two nesting in our
old oak tree were the last pair in the whole country.

'My dad was shocked and said he'd do all he could to look after them.

'From then on it was my job to keep watch. If a
stranger came near, I'd run to fetch Dad. Usually it
turned out to be a bird-watcher, or a traveller who'd lost
his way, but if Dad had any doubts, he'd tell the man
to clear off and not come back.'

'And what about the day your dad went off to market?' This is the scary bit, the bit Lowri likes most of all. 'What happened then, Gran?'

'Ah yes,' says the old woman, her voice dropping low. 'One fine spring morning, when Dad had taken some sheep down to Tregaron, I heard a yelling in the wood. I looked up, saw birds scattering from the trees, and ran.

'I couldn't see anyone,
but then I spotted a rope
dangling from a high branch
of the biggest oak tree.
I heard a rustling above me
and saw someone scrambling
up towards the nest. He was
trying to steal the eggs!'

'But why was he shouting,
Gran?' asks Lowri, her eyes
wide. 'Was he trying to
frighten the birds?'

16

'They were frightening him, more like!
They were swooping all around, trying
to stop him reaching the nest, and he
was screaming at them to keep off.

'*Leave them alone!* I yelled, at the top of my voice. And he was so surprised that he must have lost his grip, what with the kites attacking him from above and me roaring at him from below.

'*Help*, he cried, *I'm falling!* And he started crashing down, through the branches.'

'What did you do, Gran? Weren't you afraid he'd land on top of you?'

'I took hold of the rope and swung it out under him as he fell, crying, *Grab it! Grab the rope!* And he did.'

'You saved him, Gran? You saved his life?'

'Well, he still clattered to the ground, but he managed to catch hold of the rope and it slowed him down all right. Without it, he'd have broken a bone or two, I can tell you that, cariad.'

'What did you say to him, Gran? Did you give him a row?'

'I certainly did. *What do you think you're doing?* I shouted. *You're lucky you didn't break your neck!*

'*I know*, he said, groaning as he picked himself up off the ground. I nearly felt sorry for him then – he was no more than a boy, really.

'*A man said he'd give me five pounds an egg. My dad's out of work, and we need the money.*

'*Well, it isn't right!* I yelled at him. *There'll be no kites left if people like that have their way. Now clear off before my own dad catches you! Clear off and don't come back!*

'*Fair enough,* said the boy, nodding. *There must be better ways of making money. Oh, and thanks, girl,* he added, with a shy little smile. *Thanks for holding out the rope.*

'He hobbled off down the track and we never saw him again.'

'What did my Great Granda say when he came back, Granny?'

'At first I don't think he really believed me,' she replies. 'Not till I took him down to the woods and showed him the rope. The first thing he did was cut it down. And then he was angry with me, for trying to stop a thief on my own, and proud of me all at the same time.'

'So no one shot her or poisoned her or stole her eggs,' Granny says, coming towards the end of her story. 'And the last red kite in Wales had two chicks. She came back to the same nest each year from then on, knowing it was safe. Soon the young she'd hatched were making their own nests, having their own chicks and spreading further and further across the hills and forests.

'So that by now, Lowri fach . . .' Granny leans over to grab the last ginger biscuit before her granddaughter gobbles the lot, 'there might be as many as a thousand red kites in Wales!'

'But do nasty people still kill them and steal their eggs, Gran?'

'I'm afraid so, cariad. It still happens every year, but more and more of us protect them and watch out for them. The people of Wales are proud of their red kites, and proud to have helped them survive.'

And the proudest of all is Lowri, for without Granny Sarah there would be no more red kites.

Yes, without Granny Sarah and her father, the children of Wales could never again stand on a hillside and feel their spirits soar as they watch those magnificent birds flying free above the treetops, twisting and gliding in the swirling of the wind.

About the Red Kite

Red kites were once regarded as pests. Just over a hundred years ago, they had been completely exterminated in England and Scotland, and had died out almost entirely in Wales.

As it says in the story, it is believed that at one time there was just one breeding female bird in Wales. Thanks to the efforts of a few landowners and organisations such as the RSPB (www.rspb.org.uk) and the Welsh Kite Trust (www.welshkitetrust.org), there are now around 500 breeding pairs in Wales. There are about another 500 across England and Scotland, where the birds have recently been re-introduced.

Red kites nest in high trees, pairing for life and normally raising two or three chicks each spring. Because they have been protected so successfully, they were voted Bird of the Century in 1999 and made the National Bird of Wales in 2000.

If you know where to look and what to look for, it is hard to travel through mid Wales without catching a glimpse of these elegant birds, with their reddish-brown bodies and long, deeply-forked tails.

You have a very good chance of seeing them at the following Red Kite Feeding Stations:

Gigrin Farm, near Rhayader

Llanddeusant, near Llangadog

Bwlch Nant yr Arian, Ponterwyd, near Aberystwyth

Pont Einon, Cors Caron, near Tregaron

The red kites of Wales have recently spread over the border into Herefordshire and Shropshire. They also have been successfully re-introduced to the following areas of England: Wiltshire, East Midlands, Yorkshire, Tyne and Wear and the Chilterns.

The kites of Rockingham Forest, Northamptonshire can be seen on live webcam at www.forestry.gov.uk.

In Scotland there are now kites in Dumfries & Galloway, Central Scotland and Northern Scotland (in the Black Isle area). There are feeding stations in Argaty, near Stirling, and Bellymack Hill Farm, near Laurieston, Galloway.